Sort it Out!

By Barbara Mariconda
Illustrated by Sherry Rogers

Today Timmy turtle and I played in the rain

with my locket, diary and new umbrella.

For Tom Lynch who helps me sort out and stand in the mysteries of life, and Mary Santilli who taught me that everything is, in some way, about math and science!—BM

For my Grandma Askew who in my eyes was as perfect as a human can be and who I cherished and miss so much—SR

Pack rat collected a whole bag of stuff.
His mother said, "Packy, enough is enough!

Empty that stuff you've collected today!
Then sort it all out and put it away!"

A turtle, a locket, a marble, a book,
an acorn, a needle are all things that he took!

An egg, an umbrella, a brush, and some thread
are just some of the things he spilled out on his bed!

A kettle, a pinecone, some yarn, and a clover
are more of the things Packy had to look over.

A string bean and cherry were in his collection,
with pieces of sandpaper for his inspection!

But before he could put all these treasures away,
he grouped them with things that they're like in some way!

He sorted them this way and that way and then,
he looked them all over and sorted again!

The turtle, the clover, the skinny string bean,
he placed in a pile made of things that are . . .

The turtle, the egg, and the acorn that fell,
these are all things with a hard outer . . .

The acorn, the pinecone, the cherry you see,
all of these things can be plucked from a . . .

The cherry, the marble, the yarn tightly wound,
these are examples of things that are . . .

round

The yarn, the needle and thread are, you know,
all things that we use when we knit, stitch, or . . .

sew

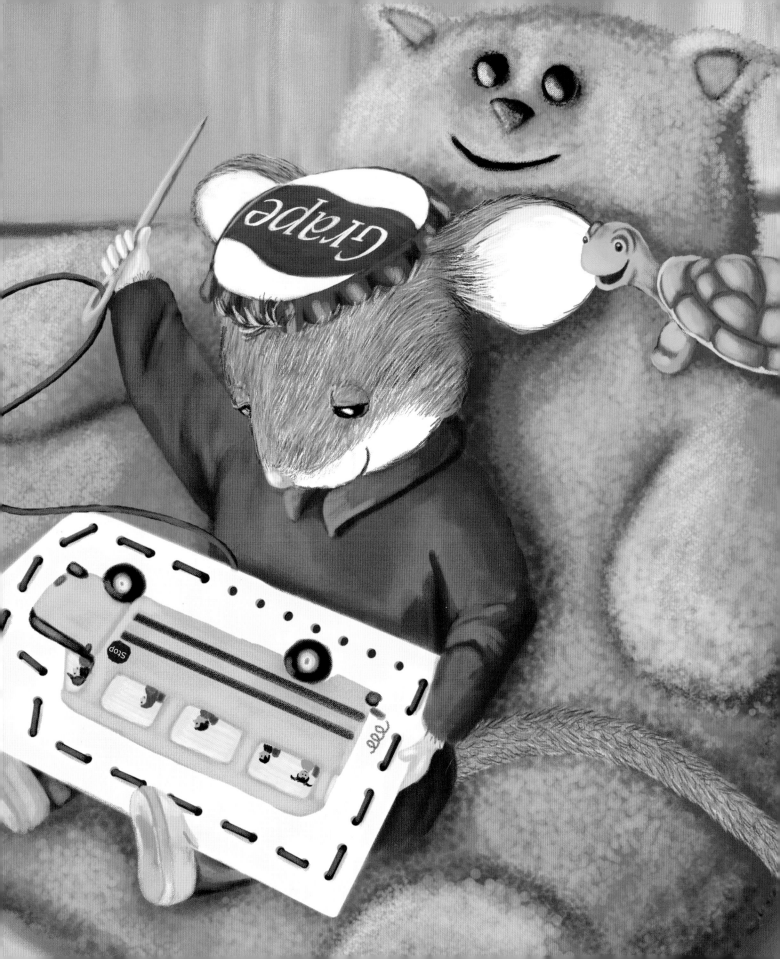

The needle, the locket, the dented tin kettle,
all these three things have been made out of . . .

Today Timmy turtle and I played in the rain with my locket, diary and new umbrella.

The locket, umbrella, and book that he chose,
these are all things you can open and . . .

The sandpaper, pinecone, and brush sure enough are all some things that feel scratchy and . . .

Rough

Still, as he sat in his room full of clutter,
shaking his head, Packy started to mutter.

He scratched at his head, and said, "I've been thinking;
why does it seem my collection is shrinking?"

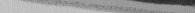

"My kettle is missing, my umbrella and book!
The egg and the cherry, my yarn—Mom, come look!"

She shrugged and she shoved all his stuff in a heap,
all of the stuff he intended to keep.

But then, how surprising, when mother was through
they discovered his red-checkered bag was gone, too!

For Creative Minds

Hidden Picture

How many items can you find hidden in the first page of the story: alphabet blocks, dominoes, buttons, pencils, paper clips, thimble, tinker-toy wheels, buttons, bottle cap, and marbles. *What are some of the other items you see in the book that Packy has collected?*

Sorting, Categorizing, and Classifying

People sort collections in different ways all the time. Laundry gets sorted into light and dark clothes or into cotton versus permanent press. This is called "sorting by attributes." An attribute is a characteristic shared by the items you group together.

Copy or print from our website and cut out "Packy's Sorting Cards." See how many different ways you can sort them. Cards may be copied using a reduction and/or an enlargement in order to provide for another aspect of size sorting.

Did you come up with different ways to sort Packy's collection?

What attributes did you use to sort the items? Describe what makes the groups different. What makes the groups similar?

Was it easy to sort everything into a few groups?

Can you make smaller groups within bigger groups?

Were there some items that didn't seem to fit into any group or that fit into more than one group? If so, what did you do with them?

Describe or explain your sorting methods to someone.

Take a survey by asking family members, friends, and classmates which collection is their favorite. List the groups in order from most favorite to least favorite.

Scientists sort things into groups too

The first question that scientists ask is whether something is "living/once-living" or "non-living." If it is living, it can be sorted into different groups called "kingdoms," which include plants or animals among others. *Can you sort Packy's things into either non-living, plant, or animal?*

- Look at the piles and guess which group has the most.
- Then count how many are in each group.
- Color a box for each item in the appropriate section of the copied/downloaded graph.
- Which one has the most? Did you guess correctly? Which has the least?

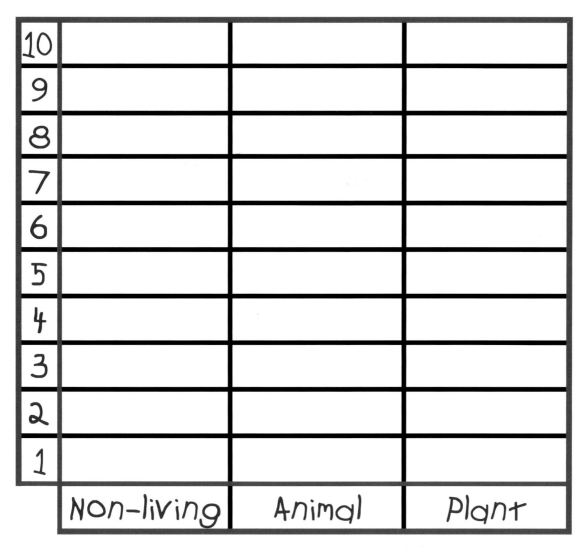

	Non-living	Animal	Plant
10			
9			
8			
7			
6			
5			
4			
3			
2			
1			

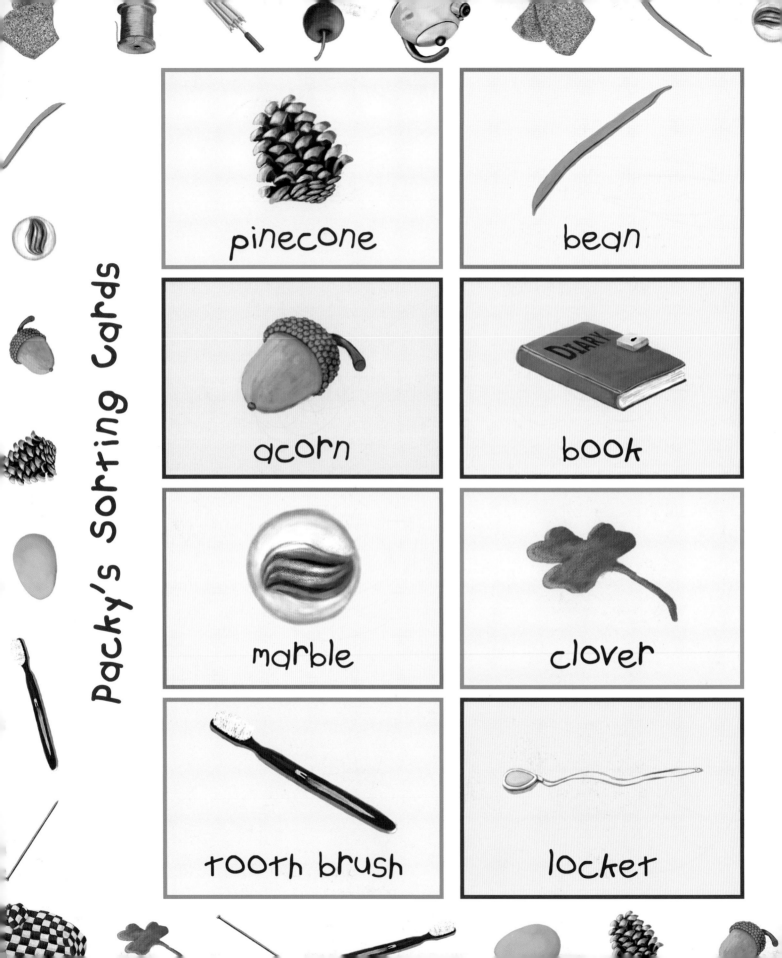

Packy's Sorting Cards

pinecone

bean

acorn

book

marble

clover

tooth brush

locket

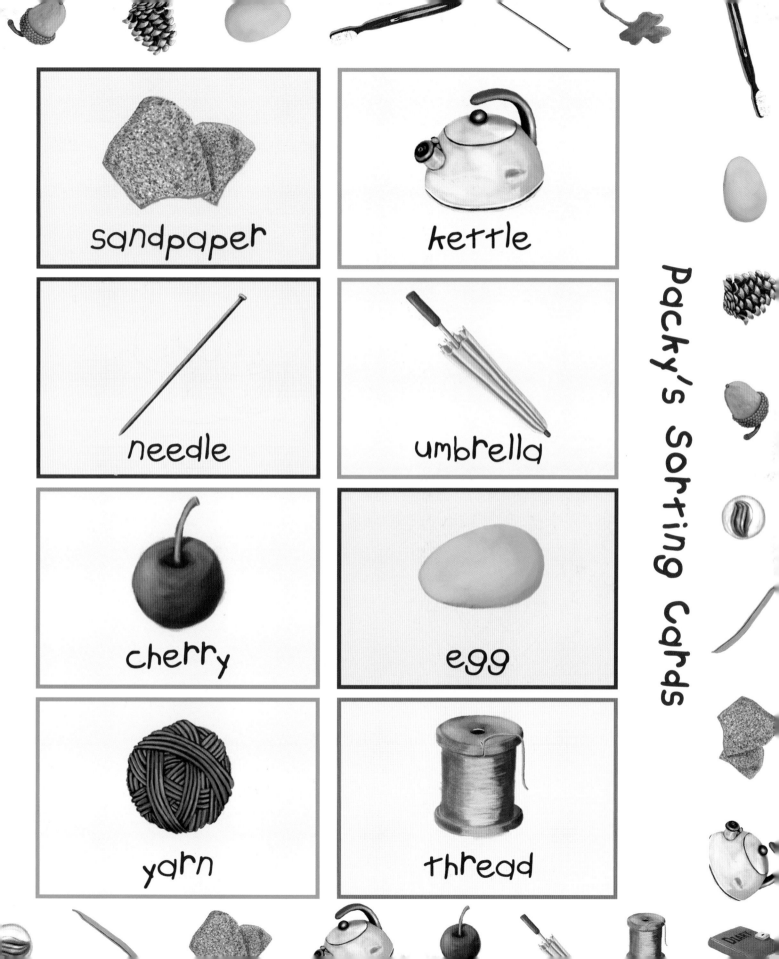

sandpaper

kettle

needle

umbrella

cherry

egg

yarn

thread

Packy's Sorting Cards

Writing Connection:

Authors use words to paint pictures! The words they choose help readers visualize and imagine the important things they are writing about. One way authors do this is to refer to important things in a variety of ways. They think about the characteristics of characters, settings, and objects and use these characteristics in their description. Let's look at some of the important objects Packy sorted and see if we can name them in a number of ways!

Example—Marble: small glass orb, miniature crystal ball, small round colorful globe

Can you think of another interesting way to say "marble"?

Try to use "word referents" for the following important objects Packy collected. One idea for each has been provided for you.

Clover	lucky four-leafed plant	_____
Turtle	armored creature	_____
Acorn	squirrel snack	_____
Cherry	ice cream sundae topper	_____

Now that you've got the hang of it, try this skill when you write or tell a story!

Publisher's Cataloging-In-Publication Data

Mariconda, Barbara.
Sort it out! / by Barbara Mariconda ; illustrated by Sherry Rogers.
p. : col. ill. ; cm.
Summary: A rhyming story about a packrat who enjoys sorting his collection of trinkets in a variety of ways.
Includes "For Creative Minds" section with sorting activities.
Interest age level: 004-008.
Interest grade level: P-3.
ISBN: 978-1-934359-11-2 (hardcover)
ISBN: 978-1-934359-32-7 (pbk.)
1. Set theory--Juvenile fiction. 2. Child collectors--Juvenile fiction. 3. Brothers and sisters--Juvenile fiction. 4. Set theory--Fiction. 5. Child collectors--Fiction. 6. Brothers and sisters--Fiction. 7. Stories in rhyme. I. Rogers, Sherry. II. Title.
PZ7.M37 So 2008
2007935086
[E]

Text Copyright © 2008 Barbara Mariconda
Illustration Copyright © 2008 Sherry Rogers
The "For Creative Minds" educational section may be copied by the owner for personal use or by educators using copies in classroom settings.

Printed in China
Sylvan Dell Publishing
976 Houston Northcutt Blvd., Suite 3
Mt. Pleasant, SC 29464